THE AMAZING ADVENTURE OF EDWARD AND DR. SPRECHTMACHEN

— A Novel —

Bob Zeidman

To Random, Darwin & Theory,
Have great adventures!

BZ
3/20/2016

Swiss Creek Publications
Cupertino, CA

CHAPTER ONE

Edward was a young boy, about nine and a half years old, who was pretty much like any other nine-and-a-half-year old boy you've ever met. He did the same things - he went to school, he watched T.V., he usually forgot to make his bed in the morning, and sometimes refused to eat his peas at dinner. He didn't like girls, at least that's what he said, and he wanted to be a fireman when he grew up. There was one thing, though, that was a little different. He had a hobby. More like an obsession. He liked to collect things. Now lots of little boys like to collect things, but Edward *really* liked to collect things. All kinds of things. Bent, rusty nails he found on the ground. Caps from old pop bottles. Wrist watches in the grass in the park. Curb feelers by the curb. Egg beaters from the neighbor's trash. Rusted bicycle chains, small electric motors, broken toasters, pocket calculators, big electric motors, fans,

1

toy guns, stretched out springs, lamp shades, nail clippers, rubber bands, rings, pencils, and rubber stamps. Just about anything, actually. And he proudly kept it all in a big shack in his back yard. When he found something interesting, and he did so almost everyday, he'd bring it home, take it apart, scrub it clean, put it back together, and carefully put it in the correct place in his shack. Everything had its correct place in his shack. Everything was organized. Things that whirred or buzzed were kept in the back left corner, second and third shelves. Things that spun or flipped belonged in the back right corner, first shelf. Things that were round with spikes lay on the fifth shelf, front left. Hairy things on the right side, second shelf. Slimy and gooey things on the table in the near left corner. And things that fell into no category at all were on the floor, right smack in the center.

The Amazing Adventure

One morning, Edward climbed up on the roof of his shack to check for leaks, because the rainy season was coming and although there had never been a leak in the shack, as far back as Edward could remember, he checked every year just to make sure. As he sat on the roof, after his inspection (there were no visible leaks) his eyes caught a glimpse of something sparkly and bright yellow in the yard of the house next to his. He squinted to see what it was, but it was too far to make out. But as the sun glanced off it, brilliant yellow dots were thrown in all directions. He had to find out what it was. So he carefully climbed down from the shack and went over to the wooden fence that separated the two houses. Jumping up, he grabbed onto the top of the fence and, with all his might, he strained and pulled and pulled and strained until his eyes were just over the top of the fence.

Now, Edward lived in a very nice house in a

very nice neighborhood. It wasn't too big and it wasn't too small, his house. There was just enough room for his mom and dad and his baby sister. The house always looked nice since his mom was always washing the windows and cleaning the window sills, sweeping the driveway and watering the lawn, planting new flowers and brushing off cobwebs. His dad was always mowing the lawn and trimming the hedges, fixing the shutters and painting the trim, raking the leaves and washing the fence.

The house next door, however, was a different matter. The house next door was covered top-to-bottom with a thin film of grey-black soot. The windows were streaked with grey-white smudges or hidden by grey-green wooden planks. Grey-brown vines crept down the sides in the dark grey cracks of the light grey bricks. Blue-grey cobwebs hung from the corners and crevices. Brown-grey weeds, five feet tall, filled the entire yard so that there wasn't even a path

from the sidewalk to the front door. And
orange-grey smoke clouds coughed out of the
red-grey chimney.

Out of the house, twenty-four hours a day, came
all sorts of mysterious noises. There were
bangs and plops and fizzes and whirrs and
jingles and clanks and pops and burps. There
were loud slams and quiet buzzes, big crashes
and little plinks, tremendous zoings and teensy
blips.

Perhaps most mysterious about the house was its
single, solitary resident. No one really knew
who he was. Some said he didn't even exist.
Others said he was a ghost or a magician. Some
said he was seven feet tall with hair that
sprung out from his head like white fire and
red laser-beam eyes. Others said that he was
only a foot tall, like an elf, with a hunched
back and claws for hands. Most people in the
neighborhood had never seen him, but everyone

knew someone that had. An uncle's friend's doctor had examined him once and found he had no heart! A friend's cousin's baby-sitter has seen him on the roof of his house at midnight dancing and singing magic incantations. A friend's friend's friend caught him shopping in the supermarket and loading his basket with newt eyes and snake gizzards.

All of this went through Edward's mind as his hands clenched the fence and his arm muscles knotted and the wood dug into his palms. But he felt none of it, so enraptured was he by the object before him.

The owner of the house, this magician or ghost or elf, was not, as you may have guessed, a very tidy person. His trash and garbage would pile up day after day, week after week, in a big heap in his back yard until early one morning it would mysteriously appear at the curb to be taken away by the garbage collectors. Occasionally it would be there a day early, and Edward had found many additions to his wonderful collection in those cans by the curb. But usually, they were out and gone before he was up, and he often wondered what treasures he had missed. This time, what Edward saw on the top of this mound as he hung from the fence was too intriguing, too magical, to let be crushed and mangled and forgotten in the belly of a garbage truck. What he saw was a large glass ball, about the size of a basketball, covered with bright yellow sparkles. Connected to it, about the size of a paper towel roll, was a silver coil that twisted and turned. On the other side of the silver coil was a dark blue cube, the size of a small tissue box, with bright red and green splotches on it. Amid the grey surroundings and sitting on top of the heap of garbage, this thing, whatever it was, looked like the royal jewels. This pirate's treasure, he thought, would be the crown of his collection, if only he could have it.

Edward slipped down from the fence and massaged his aching arms and thought. "I must have that thing, but I'm sure it'll go into a garbage can and be hauled out and picked up some morning at dawn." "I could wait every morning," he thought, but then realized he couldn't possibly wait every morning. It might be weeks before it was put out. He thought some more. "I'll just go take it. I'll take it from off of the heap," he thought. "You can't take something that doesn't belong to you," he countered. "But it's only garbage," he argued back, "it's o.k. to take something that someone doesn't want. Isn't it?" The debate went back and forth for some time but after all the arguments he just couldn't get the picture of this wonderful thing out of his mind. He decided. He would venture out to the heap, secretly, and retrieve it. He never thought to ask the man who lived there if he could have it. You just don't ask an evil sorcerer for his magic wand, even if he is throwing it out.

So Edward prepared himself for his terrible quest. He put on his heavy hiking boots - the ones with the plastic cleats on the bottom. On his head he wore his hard, safari helmet. A canteen of water and a pocket of chocolate bars for nourishment. And of course a machete to cut through the overgrowth. He set out.

He rounded the fence and stood on the sidewalk facing the grey house with its grey windows and its grey jungle of weeds. His heart beat just a little faster, but he took a deep breath, tensed his muscles, raised his machete, and entered the yard.

Through the growth he pressed forward, his eyes darting from side to side, up and down, preparing himself for thunderbolts or spears. Time went slowly as he slashed through the

mighty weeds, his feet pressing down on
hardened mud and rocks. His heart pounded in
his ears. Sweat began to trickle down from his
hair into his eyes, and it burned, but still he
continued forward, determined. Finally, the
weeds cleared, and before him he saw the trash
heap, huge, reaching skyward, with the thing
resting delicately on top. Edward was overcome
with excitement and he dropped his machete and
ran to the heap, jumping onto it and grabbing
hold with his hands as he began climbing
upward. Upward he went through old tires and
broken radios. Through moldy bread loaves and
black banana peels. Through clumps of slimy
tissue paper and bowls of forgotten oat meal.
Higher and higher he climbed, his eyes never
leaving the yellow ball with the coil and the
box that seemed to beckon him at the peak.
Finally, with his feet dug into the heap and
one hand holding onto an old electric cord, he
reached up with his other hand and plucked the
thing from the top of the heap. He brought it

down to his face and examined it with glee. The yellow was the yellowest yellow he'd ever seen. The silver coil reflected his face, and the blue box looked like the night sky.

He didn't know how long he had sat there and admired his thing - for it was his thing now - but he knew that he had to leave quickly. He had gotten what he had come for, but his journey was not yet over. He still had to escape back to the safety of his own home. Realizing this, he quickly sat and slid down the side of the heap. He slid over worn-out boots and burned-out light bulbs. Over wads of chewing gum and giant dust balls. Over pointy things and scratchy things and all sorts of unrecognizable sticky things until he reached the bottom and ran for the weeds.

What Edward didn't know was that all this time he had been watched by tiny little eyes all around the house. Not human eyes. Not animal

11

eyes. Electronic eyes that sensed his presence and set off an alarm deep within the house. As Edward reached the weeds, he tripped and fell and the thing went rolling. On his belly, he crawled, over to the thing, and placed his hands on it. But when he pulled it to him, he saw before his face, two shoes solidly planted before his nose. His heart jumped (for a moment he thought it had stopped) and he looked up to see a very short but powerful-looking man with dark chocolate skin and white hair like cotton balls teased out in every direction. The man stood with his hands on his hips, looking down at Edward, sprawled out on the ground. For a moment, Edward thought to reach for his machete, but luckily he had dropped it earlier, because he didn't know what he should do with it if he had it. Instead he just looked up and clutched his beautiful thing.

In a deep, booming voice, the man looking down at him said, "Vat are you doink?" Edward trembled but said nothing. "Vat are you doink mit my transgropulator?"

Edward cleared his throat and squeaked out, "You threw it away."

"You vant the transgropulator?" Edward nodded his head. "It doesn't verk, you know. The telesnerter is burned out." Edward continued looking at the man. "You don't know ver I can get anodder von, do you?" Edward shook his head. "Vell, you can keep dis von. You tell me if you find von dat verks, ja?" Edward nodded. "Good. Haf a good day, den," said the man and he began to walk away.

Edward watched the man walk toward the house, open the front door, and walk inside. Just before the door closed, Edward jumped to his feet and shouted, "What does it do?" then quickly covered his mouth. What had he done? He had perhaps just escaped death or something worse. The strange little man had just let him go, for who knows for what reason, and now he had called him back. Back to who knows what fate? But Edward's curiosity was greater than his fear, and he stood his ground as the little man, who it appeared was no bigger than Edward himself, turned around and walked briskly over.

"Shhhh..." said the little man, his finger rigid against his mouth. "You really vant to know?"

Edward nodded.

"You must keep a secret denn," said the little man into Edward's ear. "Can you keep a secret?"

Edward's heart filled with pride as he realized he was soon to share in some important secret. "Of course, I can keep a secret," said Edward. "When Sally told me she had cut up mom's new dress, I kept that secret. When I saw Jimmy draw that funny picture of Miss Denkler on the blackboard I kept that secret. When Tommy threw that stone through your window I kept that secret. I never tell secrets. Even if I'm tortured. Even if they were to hang me upside down by my toe nails. Even if they were to pluck my eyebrows out, one hair at a time, and force me to eat Lima beans. Even if..."

"Good," interrupted the man, "denn I can trust you mit my secret. Come inside my house. But first..." His voice rose and he shook a finger at Edward. "I cannot invite a stranger into my house. Ve must be introduced!" He extended his hand. "My name is Dr. Sprechtmachen."

Edward hesitated, then grasped his hand and shook it firmly. "I'm Edward."

"Good, Edward. Now ve can go inside and I can share my secret." With that, Dr. Sprechtmachen put his arm around Edward, and they both headed toward the house.

CHAPTER TWO

Edward followed Dr. Sprechtmachen through the
weeds to the front door. Dr. Sprechtmachen
pulled out a big, long, old-fashioned key, put
it in the door and turned it. There was a
click. Then another, then quickly another and
another. Then a few buzzes and beeps. A light
flashed in their faces. Then silence. Dr.
Sprechtmachen firmly grasped the doorknob and
turned it. He opened the door, and as they
entered, Edward saw that it was a beautiful
house on the inside. It was spotlessly clean
and mostly white with fine lacy drapes and
plush, snow-white carpets. There were
luxurious, leather couches and finely carved
metal lamps. Somehow it looked bigger than the
small, dirty house next door to him.

Dr. Sprechtmachen waved Edward over into the
kitchen, a small room with a marble floor like
vanilla fudge swirl. "A glass of hot chocolate,

17

perhaps?" asked Dr. Sprechtmachen. Edward nodded yes, still taking in the beautiful marble floor through the delicate glass kitchen table.

Dr. Sprechtmachen brought over two fine china cups of steaming hot chocolate and set them on the table. The two of them sipped their chocolates, talking about many things - about the beginnings of the post-impressionist movement in art, about organic chemical bonding and its use in bubble gum, about ray tracing algorithms in video games. Mostly it was Dr. Sprechtmachen who did the talking while Edward sipped his chocolate and fidgeted. Finally, when he could stand it no more, Edward said, "So what's your secret." Then embarrassed, he added quietly, "please."

Dr. Sprechtmachen finished his chocolate, then leaned over close to Edward and said, "Would you like to see it?"

"Of course, of course, of course," thought Edward, but instead he replied politely, "Yes, I would."

Dr. Sprechtmachen led Edward out of the kitchen and down a long hallway to a closet. He opened the door and the closet was filled with worn-out, old coats. He walked into the closet, squeezing between a dusty parka and an old tweed jacket and motioned for Edward to follow. Edward squeezed himself between a long, black overcoat and a torn up windbreaker. Dr. Sprechtmachen closed the door and switched on the light switch. Only nothing happened. The closet remained pitch black. Dr. Sprechtmachen looked down at his watch and counted. Edward was beginning to think that maybe it wasn't such a good idea to follow this strange, little man into his wonderful, strange house. He tapped Dr. Sprechtmachen on the shoulder, ready to tell him that he thought it was time he went

back home before his parents began to worry.
But Dr. Sprechtmachen shrugged off Edward's tap
and, his eyes frozen to his watch, said, "Just
one moment, just one moment," after which he
switched the switch off again. This time a loud
thunk was heard, and Dr. Sprechtmachen smiled.
He opened the door to reveal, not the hallway
they had entered from, but a staircase. Dr.
Sprechtmachen threw the switch once more, and a
light came on to light up the staircase. He
bounded down the stairs, and Edward slowly
followed.

What he saw below the house amazed him. This
room went about a hundred feet below the
ground. On the sides were all sorts of flashing
lights and spinning wheels and switches and
handles and knobs. There were also video games
with colored shapes and lines and flashing
numbers. And in the middle of this grand room
was a big red thing that looked like a giant's
ice cream cone that had fallen, ice cream side

down, right in the middle of Dr.
Sprechtmachen's house.

"This," said Dr. Sprechtmachen proudly, "is my
secret," pointing to the red ice cream cone.

"Great-o," said Edward. "It's big." He thought
some more. "It's red, too." He looked toward
Dr. Sprechtmachen. "It's terrific." Dr.
Sprechtmachen beamed. Edward thought. "What is
it?"

Dr. Sprechtmachen, who by now had reached the
bottom of the stairs, began to dance happily
around the giant ice cream cone. "This," he
proclaimed, "is my rocket ship." He danced some
more. "This," he said again, "is vat vill take
me - und you too if you vant - into outer
shpace!"

"Great-o," said Edward who had by this time
also reached the floor and joined Dr.

Sprechtmachen in his crazy dance until they were both exhausted.

Then Dr. Sprechtmachen, out of breath, leaned back against the rocket and slid to the ground. "Unfortunately," he said between gasps, "the transgropulator dat you found in my back yard is the last von I had. They are very delicate things. Und expensive, too."

Edward also leaned against the rocket and slid to the ground. "Oh," was all he could think to say though he knew it wasn't too helpful.

"I could make another von if I had the right parts," said Dr. Sprechtmachen. But I haven't been able to find them all. And to tell you the truth," he leaned over toward Edward and lowered his voice, "I shpent all my money building this ting. I'm broke."

"Oh," said Edward, now disappointed that he

wouldn't go into outer space after all, and considering it very unfair. "What do you need to make another one?"

"Vat I need is a shmall umbrella - mitout the cloth, you know - mit only the metal shpokes. Und I need a dozen light bulbs, a rusty egg beater, a shmall electric motor, a bicycle tire tube, a big vooden shpoon, a thermometer, three tarnished copper pennies, a rubber galosh, und a paper clip."

As Dr. Sprechtmachen read off his list, Edwards eyes opened and his smiled widened to nearly burst off his face. He jumped up. "I have all those things. I have all those things in my collection."

"Und I could have them for my rocketship?"

"Of course. Of course."

And they sprang up and danced some more around the rocket before racing up the stairs and into the closet, then through the hall and out the front door to Edward's collection where they found all the things Dr. Sprechtmachen needed, and a few more things that they thought might come in handy on their tour of the outer reaches.

CHAPTER THREE

Edward and Dr. Sprechtmachen worked hard all day on the rocket ship. Dr. Sprechtmachen ran around like a bug in a bottle from one corner of the laboratory to another, picking up strange-looking tools and hammering on this and pounding on that. Then he would hand the tool to Edward and Edward would hammer on this and pound on that just the way Dr. Sprechtmachen had, while Dr. Sprechtmachen sat at his workbench and put together another transgropulator. Dr. Sprechtmachen wore huge glasses that plugged into the wall and glowed soft orange. In front of him he had all sorts of tools that buzzed and grinded and sparked and zapped, and he carefully manipulated each one. Edward kept hammering on this and pounding on that, occasionally stopping when a large crash would come from Dr. Sprechtmachen's workbench. Edward would look over to see bright yellow and blue sparks shooting in all directions as Dr. Sprechtmachen connected the umbrella to the egg beater or sealed the light bulbs in the rubber galosh.

All day they worked, stopping only for lunch - Dr. Sprechtmachen made wonderful baloney sandwiches - until finally as the sun stretched over the distant hills, they finished. They put down their tools, stood back, and looked at the giant, upside-down ice cream cone, and admired their work. They were so excited they couldn't think about anything else. Edward didn't even think that his mom and dad and even his little sister might be worried about where he was. All he could think about was outer space.

"Let's go!" cried Edward excitedly.

"Patience, please," said Dr. Sprechtmachen. "There is von last ting."

"What's that?"

"Supper," said Dr. Sprechtmachen. "You should never go on a long journey mitout a good meal." Dr. Sprechtmachen walked upstairs, and Edward reluctantly followed, where Dr. Sprechtmachen made the most delicious Southern fried, honey-dipped chicken with piping hot mashed potatoes and black-eyed peas which Edward snarfed down faster than a sump pump. He had been so excited he didn't realize how hungry he was.

At dinner, Dr. Sprechtmachen talked on and on about the exciting adventures he had had and all of the wonderful places he had visited, all of them on earth because this was Dr. Sprechtmachen's first trip into outer space also. Edward was frozen, mesmerized, his only movements to breathe and stuff his mouth with chicken and potatoes and peas. Finally, when they had eaten their share and washed the dishes since they didn't know when they would return and didn't want to find solid lumps of mashed potatoes cemented to their plates, they went back to the laboratory downstairs.

Once downstairs, Dr. Sprechtmachen removed from his pants what looked like an ordinary television remote control. But when he pushed the "POWER" button, a door slid up in the side of the rocket, and Edward and he stepped inside.

Like Dr. Sprechtmachen's house, the rocket looked much larger on the inside than it did on the outside. They entered a large circular room with a ladder in the center. Dr. Sprechtmachen climbed the ladder and Edward followed. Up they went, higher and higher, past lots of doors. Some doors looked so small that Edward imagined he could only fit through if he breathed out all the way. Other doors looked big enough for an elephant to get through, but of course it would probably have a hard time climbing up the ladder. At the top, Dr. Sprechtmachen aimed his

remote control and hit a button marked
"VOLUME", and a hole opened up like an eyelid.
Dr. Sprechtmachen climbed through and Edward,
of course, followed.

Inside was the cockpit where all the main
controls were. In the center, facing out toward
the big windshield at the top of the rocket,
and bolted to the wall, were two black leather
bucket seats with patches of peeling silver
tape covering holes and holding the seams
together. In front of the seats was a padded
dashboard from a '57 Buick. Dr. Sprechtmachen
climbed into one seat and Edward climbed into
the other. Dr. Sprechtmachen buckled his
seatbelt and Edward buckled his. On his remote
control, Dr. Sprechtmachen pressed a button
labelled "HORIZ" and a great groaning, grinding
noise began. Slowly, the sides of Dr.
Sprechtmachen's house split open and lowered to
the ground. Through the windshield, they could
see the sky above them. Next, Dr. Sprechtmachen

inserted a key into the ignition and gave it a turn. The powerful engines below them started up with a bellowing roar and only Edward's heartbeat sounded louder to him. A crackly voice came over the dashboard radio, announcing, "Ten, nine, eight, seven,..." until at zero, the huge craft rocked and rolled and shuddered and shook and with a lurch left the ground and went shooting through the air. Above the houses they shot, past telephone wires and birds and clouds and airplanes. Edward's face was like Silly Putty, smooshed into the seat by an invisible hand. Dr. Sprechtmachen happily beeped the horn to warn the birds and nearby airplanes, but mostly just for fun. Up and up they went, higher and higher they climbed as the earth dropped away behind them and the sun whose rays were no longer scattered around them by the planet's atmosphere, became a bright yellow bulb in the black of space. The rocket reached a steady speed and the invisible hand let go of Edward's face.

The Amazing Adventure

Edward looked out the window and proclaimed the greatest exclamation of wonder that he knew: "Great-o!" Dr. Sprechtmachen smiled. And with the stars to hypnotize them and their muscles aching and their minds filled with wondrous thoughts, their eyelids closed and they silently drifted off to restful sleep.

The Amazing Adventure

CHAPTER FOUR

Space travel is very exciting - at least for the first few days. After that, the blackness of space just looks black and the pinpoint stars are indistinguishable from each other. Except for an occasional meteorite which bumped the side of the ship (and which Edward excitedly first thought was someone knocking on the door to come in) and a few comets with their red, green, and blue flaming tails, there just wasn't much to keep oneself occupied. Dr. Sprechtmachen and Edward played lots of card games, ate plenty of tuna fish sandwiches, and sang a rousing rendition of "One Million Bottles of Beer on the Wall." Still, Edward started to get restless.

"Where are we going, anyway?" it occurred to Edward to ask one day.

"To Pluto!" replied Dr. Sprechtmachen.

"Have you been there?" asked Edward.

"No," said Dr. Sprechtmachen. "Have you?"

Edward shook his head.

"I found a brochure," said Dr. Sprechtmachen. "It looks very pleasant." He looked around and sheepishly shrugged his shoulders. "I left it at home."

So onward they went toward Pluto, the farthest planet in the solar system, playing gin rummy, eating tuna fish sandwiches, and seeing how many rounds they could sing of "Row, row, row your boat" without messing up.

Finally, after several weeks in space, just when Edward was beginning to tire of tuna fish sandwiches, Dr. Sprechtmachen pointed out the window in front of them and excitedly began beeping the horn. "There it is," he cried.

"What? Where?" asked Edward.

"There. Over there. Right in front of us. It's Pluto."

Edward strained his eyes to see. He noticed a little blue and white dot that grew slowly larger as he watched.

"Better buckle yourself in," said Dr. Sprechtmachen, and Edward did, still watching the blue and white object, now a tennis ball, then a basketball, finally filling the whole windshield. Dr. Sprechtmachen's eyebrows danced excitedly over his forehead as he held tightly onto the wheel, steering the rocketship through greenish-blue clouds toward a flashing light on the surface of the planet.

As Edward watched, he saw a little speck in

front of them that also began to grow larger.
It grew larger very quickly. It was pointed at
the front. It was coming straight at them! It
was a missile! Someone on Pluto was shooting at
them!

"Dr. Sprechtmachen! Dr. Sprechtmachen!" Edward
looked over to see Dr. Sprechtmachen with a
large map spread out in front of him, blocking
his view. The missile sped toward them. "Dr.
Sprechtmachen," he cried out, and Dr.
Sprechtmachen looked over at Edward. Edward was
looking straight ahead at the deadly object
darting toward them. His mouth was open, his
eyes were two beachballs. Dr. Sprechtmachen
also looked ahead and he froze, his hair
standing out even farther from his head than
usual. Edward twisted around, leaned over, and
grabbed the steering wheel. But it was too
late. There wasn't enough time. The missile
would hit them and blow them into dust...

But it didn't. Instead it swerved. Edward heard a loud, "honk honk honk" and saw in the windshield of the missile a large purple, skinny fellow with an angrily outstretched tendril waving in the air, yelling things about Edwards' relatives that didn't seem very nice.

"Oh my," said Dr. Sprechtmachen, looking back down at his map, "I'm afraid I've turned the wrong way down a one way airway." He held the wheel, first prying loose Edwards hands which were still gripping it tightly, and turned quickly to the left, throwing everything in the rocket over to the right. Dr. Sprechtmachen looked up, then back down at his map. "Let's see. I need to make a right turn at the third cloud."

"This is the third cloud," said Edward, recovering from his shock.

Dr. Sprechtmachen looked up from his map, then

quickly turned right, causing everything in the
rocket to slide to the left with a loud
"chshchshchsh... clang crang blang". Dr.
Sprechtmachen looked up again. "This should be
it," he announced, but Edward had some doubts.

After a few minutes, a green flashing arrow
appeared on the planet in front of them, which
pointed at a big yellow circle. Dr.
Sprechtmachen downshifted and with a bump and a
slight grinding noise, the rocket slowed down.
Putting his foot on the brake, the rocket
stopped just above the circle, flipped around,
and gently glided to the ground.

Dr. Sprechtmachen unbuckled and checked the
ship. Edward unbuckled and headed straight to
the bathroom. After making sure that everything
was O.K., Dr. Sprechtmachen grabbed their
suitcases, put one arm around Edward, whose
legs were still wobbly from their landing, and
headed down and outside to greet a new day on

The Amazing Adventure

the planet Pluto.

The Amazing Adventure

CHAPTER FIVE

A big, blue, corrugated tube snaked out of the main building, which Edward assumed was the airport, and attached itself to the rocketship. Dr. Sprechtmachen opened the door and walked through the tube with Edward close behind. There were no windows or lights in the tube, but it seemed to glow just enough so that they could see their way through it. On the other end Edward saw what looked exactly like any other busy airport with its hustling, bustling, tussling, and rustling hobnob of hoi polloi. The one exception, and it was a big exception, was that instead of big men in dark business suits and little baby girls in pony tails and skinny ladies with lots of makeup and fat boys with ketchup stains on their mouths... instead of tall women in elegant dresses and short men in jogging suits and sneakers... instead of people with two arms and two legs and two eyes and two ears... were purple creatures like the one he'd seen in the other rocket ship that he thought was a missile. Everyone was tall and thin with purple translucent skin that jiggled when they moved. They had two legs like rubber straws that wobbled and bounced as they walked. Their arms were long and thin and when they weren't carrying anything, coiled around themselves like quivering boa constrictors. There were short ones and tall ones, fat ones and thin ones, but all of them were at least eight feet tall. On their heads which looked like long purple jelly beans, were two black marbles that were their eyes. And on top of their heads, off to one side, like a wild purple daisy growing through the sidewalk, was a single antenna.

At the exit of the tube that they had just stepped out from, was an official looking Plutacian, as Edward later found out they were called. She (Edward and Dr. Sprechtmachen never did learn to tell boys from girls but decided to call the ones with high pitched voices 'she' and the ones with low pitched voices 'he')... she was holding a pen in one tentacle and a pad in the other. The badge pinned to her uniform said, "Grezzl". Without looking down, Grezzl asked, "How long do you plan to stay in Glip?"

Dr. Sprechtmachen shrugged his shoulders, "We really don't know."

"Indefinite stay," she said to herself while quickly checking boxes on the form. "And is Glip your final destination?"

Dr. Sprechtmachen again shrugged. "Don't know."

"Indefinite destination," said Grezzl, officially scribbling more notes and checking more boxes. "And the place you will be staying while you are here?"

Dr. Sprechtmachen and Edward looked at each

other. They hadn't really thought about that before. "Don't know." said Dr. Sprechtmachen again.

Grezzl wrinkled up the slit below her eyes, which was her mouth. With obvious disdain, she made more harried notes. "And I assume you know where you are from."

Edward smiled and with pride exclaimed, "The United States of America!" Then he added, "Earth."

Grezzl moved away her notepad to see Edward and Dr. Sprechtmachen beaming up at her. "Right," she said, placing the notepad again in front of her face.

"No really," said Edward, "we're from earth."

"Right," said Grezzl, "and I'm from Mars. Now where are you really from."

Dr. Sprechtmachen began patting himself rapidly all over until he found his wallet in his jacket pocket. He took it out and from it he pulled a card with his picture. "Here," he said, stretching on his toes with his arms straining to put the card on Grezzl's notepad. "Here is my driver's license."

Grezzl looked it over carefully, then looked again at Dr. Sprechtmachen and Edward who stood still smiling up at her. Her eyes widened and her eyebrows, had she had any, would have popped off her face. Her mouth shrunk to a round, dime-size hole. She turned around quickly, raised Dr. Sprechtmachen's driver's license up in one quivering purple tendril, and shouted at another official-looking Plutacian across the hall. "Pippl. Pippl. Look at this. They're from Earth!" At this, Pippl's eyes also widened and his mouth also formed a dime-size hole as he lurched on over. The crowd, which had been busily bobbling this way and that, began to slow down, stop and gather around the two of them. The crowd began buzzing with comments.

"From earth?"

"From outer space?"

"Alien monsters?"

"In a rocket ship?"

Edward and Dr. Sprechtmachen huddled closer as the tall crowd of gelatine people closed in on them.

"Have you ever seen anything like them?"

"They're not purple."

"They seem so rigid."

"Do they talk?"

"Do they talk?"

"Do they talk?"

"Yes we talk!" shouted Edward suddenly, throwing out his chest. The crowd backed up with a single, great whoosh of breath. Edward, realizing that perhaps he hadn't done the smartest thing, drew back toward Dr. Sprechtmachen. The crowd was silent. Slowly they began to draw even closer to the two of them. A smooth, purple tentacle wrapped slowly around Edward. Then another. Then one around Dr. Sprechtmachen. Then another. Then another. Then with a great noise, the two of them were lifted into the air, high above the heads of the Plutacians, and paraded around the airport.

"Hurray for the earthlings! Hurray!"

47

"Look everybody: earth people!"

"People from earth. Little people from earth."

"Hurray for the earthlings!"

And Edward and Dr. Sprechtmachen realized that this was a celebration. One of the smaller Plutacians came scampering behind the crowd, which was growing by the moment, waving their luggage wildly above its head.

CHAPTER SIX

Edward and Dr. Sprechtmachen were celebrities.
Everyone wanted to talk to the earth people.
They were given a room at the fanciest hotel in
Glip, which they found out was the name of the
country in which they had landed on Pluto. They
were taken to the fanciest restaurants in Glip
and served delicacies that tasted,
unfortunately, very much like tuna fish
sandwiches. They ate them politely, not wanting
to disappoint their hosts. They were given big
parades in the streets of big cities where
mountain-like buildings rose out of sight. They
were driven on top of a huge truck, usually
reserved for visiting kings and queens, and
which looked like a big velvet throne on
wheels. The Plutacians of Glip lined the
streets cheering and waving, their tentacles
bobbing. The cars, which looked like mailboxes
with rubber balls for wheels, and which were
all, without exception, bright green, honked

and beeped in celebration. From the windows of the tall, tall buildings, people tossed confetti and flower petals. The confetti sparkled in the lights that were everywhere on the planet. Since the sun was so far away, it didn't provide much light, and the Plutacians had put up lamps all over which they dimmed at night and brightened during the day. The flower petals were orange and gold and smelled like cotton candy and, fortunately, tasted nothing like tuna fish sandwiches.

Edward and Dr. Sprechtmachen were given big parties, where everyone would sit around a big swimming pool filled with punch. They would lie at the edge and dip in straws, sipping away while asking all about earth.

It was at one such party that a strange event occurred that would forever change the history of the planet Pluto. Edward and Dr. Sprechtmachen were lying about the punchpool, talking to President Zerp, the leader of the country of Glip who had thrown this party for them. The most important people in the country of Glip were there, all talking and sipping, when suddenly an fearful silence fell upon the crowd, starting at the front gate and working its way toward the pool. President Zerp froze and looked forward, and Edward and Dr. Sprechtmachen looked this way and that to see what the problem was. The crowd of Plutacians parted as a single Plutacian with a scroll in its hand wobbled slowly toward them. Gasps were let out as it walked by, but it kept its head straight forward and continued without slowing. It stopped finally in front of President Zerp. Several Plutacians started toward them, but President Zerp rose and held up his hand to stop them.

"Why does such a horrid creature show itself at our celebration?" said President Zerp.

The Plutacian, whose black marble eyes shone defiantly, said, "I bring a message from President Nedi of Glop." He handed the scroll to President Zerp who took it without looking at it, instead keeping his eyes on the messenger. Continued the messenger: "President Nedi of Glop declares complete and total war on the hideous inhabitants of Glip which shall not end until their ugliness is wiped completely from the planet." With that, he spun around quickly, eyes forward, and bobbled slowly back from where he came, again followed by the gasps of the crowd.

"Vat is that?" asked Dr. Sprechtmachen.

"That," said President Zerp with contempt, "is a horrible creature from the neighboring country of Glop. They are evil, deformed creatures. They dare to consider themselves Plutacians. But they are not. How can something so repulsive be anything but criminal."

Edward looked at the messenger as it walked
into the distance. He could see no difference
between it and the others at this party or any
other Plutacian he had met so far. "What is so
ugly?" he said. "He looks like everyone else."

President Zerp's body contracted into rigidity.
His face grew orange with anger. Only Edward's
celebrity status kept him from the full,
unshielded wrath of President Zerp.
"Can you not see?" he exclaimed. "Can those
small globes you call eyes not take in what is
so plain in front of you?"

Edward turned to look once again at the
messenger but still could see nothing wrong,
nothing different.

President Zerp saw Edward's confusion and burst
out, "Their antennas. Can you not see? The
wretches have their antennas on the wrong side

of their heads!"

And Edward did see, for the first time, that while the citizens of Glip had their single antennas on the right sides of their heads, the messenger had his dangling from the left.

President Zerp turned to the waiting crowd and declared, "And so shall the President of Glip declare ultimate war on the people of Glop. We shall fight gloriously until every horrible one is destroyed, and beauty and goodness once again are supreme upon the entire planet of Pluto."

CHAPTER SEVEN

The war preparations began. The happy
celebrations and carefree dancing ended.
Instead, somber lines of soldiers in dark,
stiff uniforms hup-two-threed down the empty
city sidewalks. The smiling, purple faces of
the people were changed to downcast, dreary
grimaces. The joy and happiness of Edward and
Dr. Sprechtmachen's arrival from earth were
replaced by a gloom that settled like thick,
dark smoke on the country of Glip.

Edward and Dr. Sprechtmachen went back to their
hotel room. No one wanted to have fun or sip
from punchpools because they knew the war was
soon upon them. The earth people were no longer
important celebrities because more important
matters had to be taken care of.

Edward paced back and forth in the hotel,
watching the streets below through the window.

The Amazing Adventure

The funny green cars passed in silence. No
confetti rained down from great heights.
Soldiers marched up and down, up and down the
streets, yelling their gruff soldier yells and
clacking their hard soldier boots. Edward paced
back and forth, watching.

"This is terrible!" said Edward. "This is
terrible!"

Dr. Sprechtmachen slowly combed his hair in the
mirror.

"The Plutacians of Glip have been so nice to
us. This is terrible."

Dr. Sprechtmachen said nothing but pulled
tangles from his beard and knotted his
eyebrows.

"This shouldn't happen. People will get hurt."

Dr. Sprechtmachen rubbed his face.

"We can't let this happen. Can't we do something?"

Dr. Sprechtmachen raised his hand slowly and waved it about in front of his face, watching it very closely.

Edward spun around and looked at him. "Well... Can't we do something?" he demanded. "All you do is look at yourself in that silly mirror!"

Dr. Sprechtmachen stopped waving his hand and looked at Edward in the mirror.

"Well?" asked Edward, a little more quietly and much less demanding. "Can't we do anything?"

"Maybe. Maybe ve can do something. Come here." He motioned Edward toward him, still watching him in the mirror.

Edward came closer. A smile began to break through on his face. "You have a plan, don't you?" asked Edward, grinning.

"I have a plan," replied Dr. Sprechtmachen.

"Will it work?" Edward asked.

Dr. Sprechtmachen scratched his chin and thought for a moment. "Couldn't hurt," he replied, and Edward smiled even more.

CHAPTER EIGHT

The next day, President Zerp received an urgent phone call from Dr. Sprechtmachen. "What is the matter?" asked President Zerp impatiently.

"Ve must talk to you immediately. It is a matter of great importance."

"Don't you know I am preparing for a war? For the single greatest and most devastating war to ever take place on this planet. I don't have time for important matters!"

"But Mr. President," said Dr. Sprechtmachen, "this is extremely urgent und pressing und significant. Besides, I have read something about your country, und I know that it is considered very impolite to refuse the urgent request of a visitor from another planet."

President Zerp hesitated for a moment. "You are

absolutely right. But it must be quick. I must prepare for this war!"

"Meet us at our hotel room at seven o'clock tonight." And Dr. Sprechtmachen hung up. He looked at Edward and the two of them grinned. They grasped each other's hands and gave a lone conspiratorial shake.

At seven o'clock exactly (because presidents are never late especially when meeting with visitors from other planets), President Zerp arrived at the hotel room. He knocked on the door and Dr. Sprechtmachen opened it just enough for President Zerp to squeeze his tall, skinny body through. Inside it was dark. There was only one dim bulb in the far corner of the room and President Zerp had to squint to see Dr. Sprechtmachen and Edward standing in front of a thick curtain.

"Now why did you ask me here? Make it quick

because I must immediately return to continue planning the destruction of the repulsive people of Glop."

"That is precisely vy ve have brought you here," said Dr. Sprechtmachen. "Ve feel that this var will cause much suffering of the people of both Glip and Glop. Ve do not vant this war to happen. Und so ve have brought you here to negotiate!"

"Negotiate? Negotiate with you?"

"No," said Edward, as he slowly drew back the curtain. "To negotiate with him!"

President Zerp drew a sharp breath through his dime-sized mouth. Standing on the other side of the curtain, he could see President Nedi of Glop standing in front of him. "How dare you bring this filthy being into my country and into my presence! This is a horror!" He turned to President Nedi. "You are a horror. You are a deformity of nature. You and your people."

He took a step closer and so did President Nedi, which surprised him, and he stopped. A person from Glop can never be trusted. "I shall call my guard immediately!" he cried. "They shall lock you in a dungeon until your skin rots off!"

He shook his fist at President Nedi and President Nedi had the gall to shake his own fist right back. "You can never win this war. Your people will be destroyed."

He pointed his finger at President Nedi. "And stop pointing your finger at me," he yelled, his face bright orange from anger. He took a deep breath and heard the quiet chuckles of the two earthlings next to him. But before he could vent his anger on them also, Edward turned on another light. The air that filled his chest to bursting in preparation for another tirade against his opponent, instead whistled out softly. His head lost its orange rage and reverted to a dark purple of embarrassment. His tendrils curled around his slender form as he stared in front of him, not at President Nedi as he had led himself to believe, but instead at his own reflection in the mirror. His own reflection with its antenna on the left side of his head. A reflection, that suddenly looked not nearly as gruesome as he had once thought.

President Zerp looked at the two earth people for a very long moment without saying anything. There was only silence in the room. Then finally, "I shall do my best to stop this silly war," and he slowly walked out of the hotel room. He paused at the door and looked back. "Thank you, my friends," he said, and continued out the door, down the stairs, and out of the hotel into the streets below.

President Zerp called an emergency meeting of all the politicians in the land of Glip. They all met in the Grand Governmental Palace and waited in hushed silence, wondering what important news President Zerp had for them. President Zerp appeared and told them of his encounter with the mirror. He told them how perhaps the people of Glop were not so ugly after all. That perhaps they were not so evil. That perhaps they were really not very different from themselves. He gave wonderful speeches that lasted through the night, for President Zerp was a smart man who, when someone showed that he was wrong, would work hard to correct his mistakes. He talked on and on until the morning of the next day, when finally, all of his politicians believed what he said was true. Then he did something that had never been done before. He called President Nedi directly. He told President Nedi about the mirror. He told President Nedi that he had been wrong. He told him that he didn't want war.

The Amazing Adventure

That his politicians didn't want war. That the people of his country didn't want war. President Nedi listened, then argued, then listened some more, then argued some more, and as they talked his arguments grew weaker until he too realized the truth. And the more they talked the more they found that the people of Glip and the people of Glop had in common. The people of Glip and the people of Glop liked to drink their Glugglug juice with two cubes of sugar and a twist of Drimmle. They both liked to play drummal-ball on the weekends and listen to twee-erp music. And most of all, both the people of Glip and the people of Glop liked to have great parties with lots of punchpools.

So on the next day, when the war was supposed to happen, instead there was a great holiday. There were parades and speeches. There was dancing in the streets and sipping by the punchpools. There was laughing and singing. And right-heads and left-heads laughed and sang and danced together as if there was no difference between them. And there really wasn't.

And Edward and Dr. Sprechtmachen slipped back to their rocketship and left the planet Pluto. They were very happy with what they had helped to do, and didn't mind that with all the celebrations, the people of Pluto had forgotten them. But they were wrong. The people of Pluto had not forgotten them. Because today, on what was once a dirt path between Glip and Glop, there is now a busy highway between the two countries. And on either side of this highway are two great statues - taller than any others on the entire planet of Pluto. They are of the two greatest heros in the history of the planet - Edward and Dr. Sprechtmachen.

CHAPTER NINE

In the ship, Edward and Dr. Sprechtmachen played more card games, ate more tuna fish sandwiches, and talked on and on about the wonderful things they had seen and the great friends they had made on Pluto. They had decided to head back home, and things were pretty peaceful aboard the "Butter Pecan" which is the name Edward had given the great ship in honor of his favorite ice cream flavor. Things were peaceful, that is, until in the middle of one particularly exciting game of gin rummy, as Edward reached for the three of hearts which would have completed a set and given him a definite lead over Dr. Sprechtmachen, Edward gasped and froze. Dr. Sprechtmachen jumped up and looked around the ship, frightened.

"Vat? Vat is it?" cried Dr. Sprechtmachen.

"My folks," replied Edward.

"Vere? Vere?" asked Dr. Sprechtmachen, peering in the corners, looking for Edward's folks.

"Back home. My folks back home. I've been gone for weeks. They must be going crazy. I didn't leave them a note or anything. When I get back they'll ground me for the rest of my life. No television for fifty years. I'll be sent to my room without dinner for the next month. I should never have gone to Pluto without telling them."

Dr. Sprechtmachen relaxed and sat down. "Not to worry. Everything vill be ok."

"That's easy for you to say. You probably told your mom and dad that you'd be gone to Pluto. I didn't." And Edward began to shake, anticipating what would happen when he got back home. Dr. Sprechtmachen came over to him and put his arm around Edward to calm him down.

The Amazing Adventure

Then he began explaining to Edward something about Einstein's relatives and Speedo Lite. Edward didn't really understand, but Dr. Sprechtmachen's deep, slow voice soothed him and his shaking stopped.

"Und so," finished Dr. Sprechtmachen, "venn ve return home, not a single moment vill have passed from the time ve left."

"You mean, it will be exactly the same time?"

"Exactly. Not one second vill have passed."

"Even though we spent weeks away from the earth..."

"It will be dinner time, that same day that you first saw my broken transgropulator."

Edward was silent for some time as he thought about this. It didn't make much sense, but Dr.

Sprechtmachen had been right all along, so he picked up the three of hearts, made his set, and went on to win one of the best gin rummy games he had ever played.

After 732 more games of gin rummy, 53 tuna fish sandwiches, 66 games of checkers, 63 glasses of grape juice, 112 games of rock, paper, scissors, and one argument about who was the greatest baseball player of all time, the rocketship "Butter Pecan" touched down squarely in the basement of Dr. Sprechtmachen's house. Edward looked at his wristwatch and, sure enough, it was the same day he had left.

"Vell," said Dr. Sprechtmachen, "it has been a great adventure and a vonderful journey."

"Yes it has," said Edward, feeling a little sad for some reason.

"But now it is time to rest," said Dr.

Sprechtmachen, "and prepare for our next trip."

"Our next one?" said Edward, perking up.

"Of course," said Dr. Sprechtmachen.

"When?" said Edward.

"Ven? Ven we have rested." Dr. Sprechtmachen looked up at the "Butter Pecan." "And ven ve have fixed up the 'Butter Pecan' so that she is ready for her next voyage."

Edward looked up at the "Butter Pecan" now with even more awe than when he had first seen it. Dr. Sprechtmachen walked over to his workbench, picked up the broken transgropulator which had started this whole adventure, and handed it to Edward.

"Don't forget this," said Dr. Sprechtmachen.

"I won't," said Edward, "I won't forget any of this."

Then Edward ran up the long staircase, into the closet, closed the door and flicked the switch, then opened the door and darted through the hallway, past the kitchen, into the living room, out the front door, and through the tall weeds of Dr. Sprechtmachen's wonderful house. He stopped at the shack in his backyard, and placed the transgropulator gently in a corner by itself. Then he dashed into his house just in time for dinner. His parents asked where he had been all day and Edward thought for a moment about all that had happened but he knew better than to try to explain that he had been to Pluto with the strange little man next door where there had been a big celebration and they had stopped a big war from happening. Instead he just answered "Out."

After dinner he went right to bed, to the

surprise of his parents who usually had to drag him to bed while he came up with the most imaginative excuses for staying up late. Instead, he tugged his clothes off, jumped into bed, pulled the sheet tightly around his neck, and thought wonderful thoughts about tuna fish sandwiches and a little dark man with cotton-white hair and purple jelly-bean people with droopy antennas and big swimming pools filled with punch, and he drifted slowly and happily off to sleep.

51560222R00043

Made in the USA
Charleston, SC
26 January 2016